Real-Life

CRIMES

... and how they were solved

Scott Singleton

Lured to her Death

Who Fired the Shot?

Murder at Madison Square Garden

UK £1.50 Republic of Ireland IR£1.75 Malta M£1.25

Real-Life CRIMES

... and how they were solved

Contents

Volume 6 Part 79

COMING IN PART 80

CRIME CASE STUDY

The Killer Who Wanted to Die: Gary Gilmore had spent most of his adult life in prison. After he was sentenced to death for two senseless murders, he fought for his right to be executed

INCRIMINATING EVIDENCE

Hair of the Dog: A young boy was found strangled to death in a quarry. Police questioned a builder, but he denied the murder. Three dog hairs found on the boy's jumper finally clinched the case

MIND OF EVIL

Eight Times a Murderer: A series of brutal murders started in Glasgow in 1956. Police suspected a local burglar. But the cunning killer eluded police for two years

Published by:
Eaglemoss Publications Ltd
7 Cromwell Road
London SW7 2HR
Circulation Manager:
Gary Neale
Subscription and Back Numbers Enquiries:
Customer Services 0424 755755

Editorial offices:
REAL-LIFE CRIMES
Midsummer Books Ltd
179 Dalling Road
London W6 0ES

Managing Editor: Stan Morse
Editors: Chris Bishop
Trisha Palmer
Production Editor: Sheryl Fellows
Design: Vanessa Stoddart
Picture Researchers: Veneta Bullen
Davina Bullen
Sophie Mortimer

Colour reproduction:
Chroma Graphics Pte Ltd, Singapore
Printed in Great Britain by: Varnicoat Ltd

HOW TO MAKE SURE YOUR COLLECTION IS COMPLETE

To be sure of getting your copies each week, either place a regular order with your newsagent or take out a subscription.

HOW TO TAKE OUT A SUBSCRIPTION

(UK and Republic of Ireland only)
We will deliver REAL-LIFE CRIMES at no extra cost. Simply write to REAL-LIFE CRIMES Subscriptions, PO Box 1, Hastings, TN35 4TJ, or telephone 0424 755755.

How to pay
You can pay by cheque, postal order or credit card, and when your subscription is due to expire a renewal letter will be sent to you asking whether you wish to continue your collection.

You may order as many copies as you like, but we suggest a minimum of 10 parts. Please include payment with your order and be sure to state the part number of the first copy you want. You can calculate the amount to pay by multiplying the cover price by the number of parts required, for example 10 issues x £1.50/IR£1.75 will cost £15/IR£17.50 (postage and packing are free).

Cheques or postal orders should be made payable to Woodgate (Eaglemoss) Ltd.

If paying by credit card, be sure to state the cardholder's name, the type of card (e.g. Access or Visa), the card number and the expiry date.

BINDERS

UK and Republic of Ireland: Binders are priced at £5.95/IR£5.95. To get your binder, send a cheque or postal order, made payable to Woodgate (Eaglemoss) Ltd, to REAL-LIFE CRIMES Binders, PO Box 1, Hastings, TN35 4TJ. For payment by credit card, telephone 0424 755755.
Australia: Binders are priced at $14.95. To get your binder, send a cheque or money order, made payable to Bissett Magazine Services Pty Ltd, to REAL-LIFE CRIMES Binders, PO Box 315, Vermont, Victoria, or telephone (03) 872 4000.

ACKNOWLEDGEMENTS

Authors: Patrick Pender
Brian Innes
Tony Wilmot
Photography: David Hendley
For their valuable help and advice, our thanks to:
Emeritus Professor Alan Usher

Picture acknowledgements
Front cover: Express Newspapers. **1725:** Rex Features/ Midsummer. **1726:** Robert Hewson/Press Association. **1727:** Cassidy and Leigh/Cassidy and Leigh/Express Newspapers. **1728:** Press Association/Cassidy and Leigh. **1729:** John Frost Newspapers/Cassidy and Leigh/Cassidy and Leigh. **1730:** Press Association/Cassidy and Leigh/Cassidy and Leigh. **1731:** Express Newspapers. **1732:** John Frost Newspapers/Press Association (three). **1733:** Express Newspapers. **1734:** Philippe Plailly-Science Photo Library/Associated Press. **1735:** Aerospace Publishing/MacClancy Collection. **1736:** UPI Bettmann/Popperfoto. **1737:** Popperfoto (all). **1738:** Aerospace Publishing. **1739:** Dr Gary S. Settles and Stephen S. McIntyre-Science Photo Library. **1740:** UPI Bettmann/Mary Evans Picture Library. **1741:** The Bettmann Archive/UPI Bettmann. **1742:** UPI Bettmann/The Bettmann Archive. **1743:** UPI Bettmann/UPI Bettmann. **1744:** UPI Bettmann/ UPI Bettmann. **1745:** Popperfoto (three)/The Bettmann Archive. **1746:** UPI Bettmann/Topham Picture Source.

LURED TO HER DEATH

SCOTT SINGLETON

Above all else, Lynne Rogers wanted a job that would allow her to travel. So when she was invited for an interview with a company operating private business jets, she jumped at the chance. But in her enthusiasm she walked into a deadly trap.

Lynne Rogers was a pretty girl who had a passion for horses. Full of energy and ambition, she was determined to succeed. The opportunity to work as an air stewardess sounded just what Lynne wanted. She was to meet her prospective employer at Charing Cross Station.

Seventeen-year-old Lynne Rogers could hardly contain her excitement as she combed her shoulder-length strawberry-blonde hair and adjusted her make-up in front of the bedroom mirror. For weeks she had been looking for a new job, something in the travel industry. Now it looked as though she had found it.

She had received a phone call from a director of a firm operating a fleet of executive aircraft. Although they had never met, he had virtually offered her the position. The job sounded great. It involved working from Gatwick Airport, training as a stewardess to chaperone business chiefs on flights overseas. There would be frequent trips to Europe, and a salary of £15,000 per year, more than double the pay at her last job as a clerk.

In a polite, well-spoken voice her prospective employer told Lynne he had seen her CV and knew she was exactly what his firm were looking for. He sounded very nice on the phone, and now she was on her way to meet him for the first time.

Charing Cross appointment

They had arranged to rendezvous at Charing Cross Station in London at 10 a.m. on the morning of Wednesday 4 September 1991. From there, he told her, they would travel to Shorham in Sussex, where they would be picked up by a helicopter and flown the short hop to Gatwick to look at the offices. She had been told to take her passport.

Left: According to the conversation she had on the phone, Lynne would be working here at Gatwick Airport. There are dozens of reputable companies based at the airport specialising in the profitable trade of business aviation charters.

Below: Lynne's father, Derek, was a 55-year-old carpenter. He had been dubious about Lynne's interview, and when she did not return that evening he was extremely worried. Together with Lynne's boyfriend he checked with all her acquaintances, but to no avail. By 10.30 p.m. he decided to contact the police.

Lynne's father, Derek, said it sounded too good to be true, and that she should be careful. The happy-go-lucky teenager just laughed and told him he worried too much. What harm could come to her in broad daylight in the centre of London or at Gatwick Airport?

Lynne put on her best black business suit over a white blouse before leaving the home she shared with her father and elder sister Suzanne in Elmer Road, Catford, south London. She drove her red Ford Escort through the rush-hour traffic to a side street near Hither Green station and boarded a train for Charing Cross.

Lynne had promised to ring her boyfriend, Spencer Clark, at lunchtime to let him know how the interview had gone. When she didn't call, he was surprised but not too concerned – there must be a good reason. But in the evening he went to her house and was shocked to find she had not returned home. Her father, a 55-year-old carpenter, was also anxious.

Determined to succeed

Lynne was a bright girl and had done well at school, gaining seven GCSE passes. Determined to better herself, she had sent copies of her CV to more than 100 employment agencies and travel firms. It was one of them, a firm based in Greenwich, south London, who had apparently supplied her details to the Gatwick company. After Lynne had left for her appointment, Mr Rogers had tried phoning them, only to find their number had been disconnected.

At 10.30 p.m., with still no word from Lynne, her father and boyfriend went to Catford police station and reported her missing. At the headquarters of Scotland Yard's Three Area Major Incident Pool, Detective Superintendent Douglas Auld read the facts listed on the missing person report with a growing sense of unease. Seventeen-year-old girls like Lynne frequently went off without warning. They had usually been swept off their feet in a whirlwind romance or walked out because of a family argument. But two things about this case troubled Auld.

The first was that Lynne was devoted to a chestnut-coloured horse called Duke. She went religiously every day to the Frogpool Manor stables at Chislehurst to feed, groom and exercise Duke. One of the reasons she wanted a better job was to help with the upkeep of her beloved pet. But Lynne had failed to turn up at the stables on Wednesday night – the first

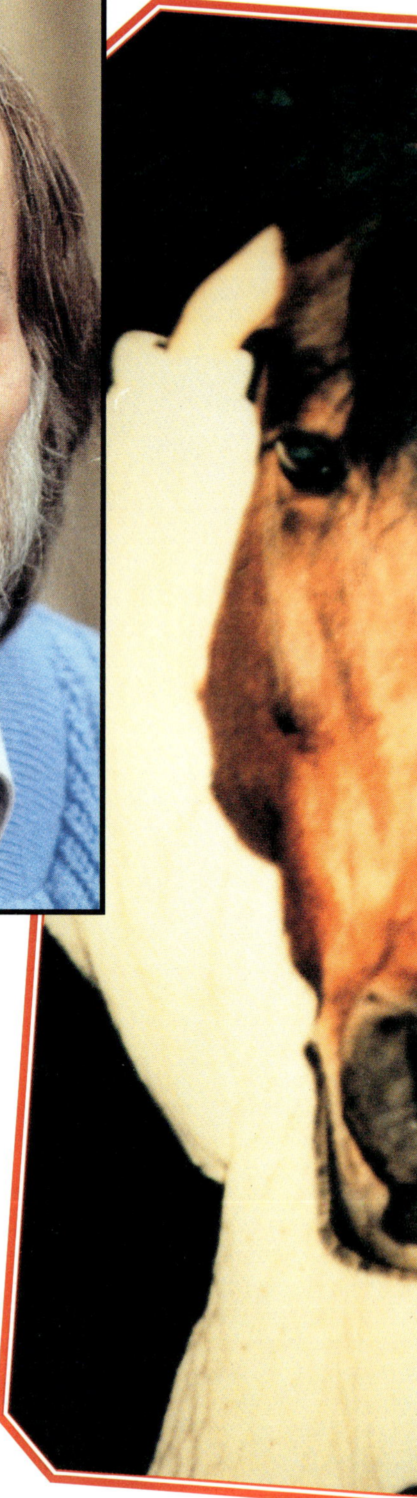

time anyone could remember her not being there.

A fishy-sounding appointment

The second worry was the account given by her father and her 19-year-old sister Suzanne of the interview appointment. Auld thought it sounded very fishy.

The detective authorised for a photograph and details of Lynne's disappearance to be circulated to the national press and TV. Later that day Lynne's car was found parked near Hither Green station.

On Saturday 7 September a press conference was organised at Scotland Yard. Derek Rogers made an impassioned plea for anyone knowing anything about the whereabouts of his daughter to come forward. The story was headlines in the Sunday papers, but still there was no news.

On Monday afternoon Auld received the message he was dreading. The body of a teenage girl had been found in a wood in Sussex; it looked like Lynne Rogers. Superintendent Auld met up with Detective Superintendent Michael Bennison of Sussex police at the murder scene.

Lynne's body lay just a few yards from a quiet country lane which led into a wood, part of the grounds of Rothersfield Manor near Rothersfield, three miles from the town of Crowborough in East Sussex. It had been discovered by local handyman John Rumens, who had been carrying out

Catford
London
SE6 2ER

Dear Sir/Madam

I have been working for a relatively small Investment and Insurance Company for about one year.

I am currently looking for a permanent position in the travel industry. I would therefore be pleased if you would consider me for a suitable position should one arise.

I enclose my CV for your perusal.

I look forward to hearing from you in the near future.

Yours faithfully,

L. G. Rogers

MISS LYNN G. ROGERS

CURRICULUM VITAE

Name: Lynne ROGERS (Miss)

Address: Catford, London, SE6 2ER

Date of Birth: 11.4.1974.

Tel No.: (Home)

Education:

Sept 1988-July 1990 — Sedgehill School, Sedgehill Road, Bellingham, London, SE6.

Sept 1985-July 1988 — Crofton Park School, Manwood Road, Catford, London, SE6.

Qualifications: GCSE :

Subject	Grade
English Language	D
Maths	E
Geography	E
English Literature	E
Office Studies Information Processing	F
Science	G
Oral communication	4

Interests: Horse riding. I own my own horse and therefore have all the responsibility of its welfare. Entering various equestrian competitions. Swimming. Ice skating and socialising.

Employment: August 1990 - Present — AYLESBURY ASSOCIATES, Investment & Insurance Brokers, 240a High Street,

Above: Lynne had been working as an insurance clerk, but had no plans to remain in that business. She had sent her CV with a covering letter to more than 100 employment agencies and firms involved with the travel industry. The man who phoned to arrange the meeting at Charing Cross had clearly seen one of those letters.

Left: Lynne's great passion in life was riding. She had her own horse called Duke, which she kept at the Frogpool Manor stables in Chislehurst. Every day she would go to the stables to feed and groom her horse. So when she did not appear on the evening after her interview, people began to worry.

hedging and ditching work alongside Rothersgate Lane.

Lynne's body had been placed in a dense patch of brambles, and leaves and branches had been hastily arranged to try to hide her. She was still fully clothed in the white blouse and black suit that she had been wearing when she set off for her interview the previous Wednesday. Her vanity case containing her purse and passport were missing.

Strangled to death

At Eastbourne mortuary a post-mortem revealed that Lynne had been strangled to death. Bruising around her throat showed where the killer had gripped her with his bare hands and choked the life out of her. Death had probably occurred less than 24 hours beforehand, on Sunday 8 September. So where had she been since Wednesday?

There were other marks on her body. A livid bruise on her forehead showed where she had been struck a forceful blow, and there were clearly visible bite marks on her chin. Lynne had not been raped, but the teeth marks seemed to indicate that her death had occurred during or shortly after some kind of frenzied attempt at sex. Perhaps Lynne had rejected her killer's amorous advances, thus sealing her fate.

Forensic dentist Bernard Grant Sims examined the deep bite injuries. He told the detectives: "The injuries are quite clear. If you can find a suspect who has a bite to match them, then you have your man." Now all the police needed was a suspect.

There were scores of leads the police had to pursue. First of all, how had the killer got hold of Lynne's name and tele-

Five days after Lynne Rogers' disappearance, a local handyman found the body of a teenage girl in a wood near Rothersfield in East Sussex, about 40 miles from Charing Cross Station where Lynne had last been seen. Police forensic experts, seen here during their search of the site, confirmed that it was Lynne. She had been strangled to death.

Lynne was found hidden in a patch of brambles a few yards off a quiet and little-used country lane. The scene of crime search is vital at any violent death, but in wooded country like this it is difficult. Here Sussex police officers make a fingertip search of every inch of the nearby ground.

DAILY MIRROR, Saturday, September 14, 1991

WISH I'D GONE WITH LYNNE, SOBS HER DAD

'I was worried by work offer'

THE WEEPING father of murdered teenager Lynne Rogers admitted yesterday: "I wish I'd gone with her."

Lynne, 17, was strangled after being lured to London's Charing Cross station last week by a man who offered her a job interview.

Her body was found four days later in a coppice at Rotherfield, East Sussex.

By GEORGINA WALSH

Head in hands, her dad Derek sobbed that after Lynne left their home in Catford, London, for the interview he wished he had gone with her.

"I obviously felt worried – and I sent her there," he added.

Derek, 49 – whose wife Jill collapsed and died three years ago – pleaded:

"I want people to keep trying to get this person so I can have my Lynne back and put her with her mum."

He told a press conference at the murder hunt HQ in East Grinstead: "It is my daughter this time. It could be someone else's next time.

Cheroots

"I'd like everyone who was in the Charing Cross area to stop and think. It's only a couple of minutes of their time."

Witnesses saw a girl like strawberry blonde Lynne meet a nervous, sun-tanned man chain smoking cheroots at Charing Cross – then get into a blue-grey C-registered Vauxhall Cavalier or Carlton.

Derek said the man who phoned Lynne with the job offer gave her a name.

"Lynne said he had mentioned it but she had forgotten it," he said.

But police revealed that Lynne kept meticulous notes of who she wrote to in search of a job and their replies.

Det Supt Michael Bennison, in charge of the hunt, said: "Obviously the killer had her CV."

DISTRAUGHT: Lynne's father Derek yesterday

STRANGLED: Lynne

LYNNE
REST IN PEACE
WE LEFT NO STONE
UNTURNED
FROM
SEARCH TEAM
MEMBERS & SOCO.

Cops' flower tribute

POLICE officers who combed the area where Lynne's body was found for clues have left this wreath at the site, with the poignant message: "Rest in peace. We left no stone unturned."

Lynne's heartbroken father and members of the public have also left flowers on the spot.

BRAVE SISTER TO HELP HUNT

BIG sister Suzanne Rogers has bravely agreed to backtrack Lynne's last known movements to help trap her killer.

The police reconstruction will be staged next Wednesday, exactly two weeks after Lynne, 17, was lured to her death.

Wearing the same style of white blouse and dark skirt as her sister, Suzanne, 18, will travel by train from Hither Green, South London, to Charing Cross station.

Police will hand passengers photofits of the suspected killer and ask if anyone saw Lynne.

Suzanne will finally walk to the spot where Lynne was last seen outside Charing Cross.

A police spokesman said last night: "Suzanne is tremendously brave to do this. It will be very difficult for her."

ORDEAL: Suzanne

Left: The discovery of Lynne's body confirmed all her father's worst fears – fears that had been with him even before she set out that fateful morning.

Witnesses remembered seeing Lynne in the company of a stocky, nervous man who was chain-smoking cheroots. They were able to provide enough information for police to issue this composite image of the man they wanted to question.

phone number? She had sent copies of her CV to over 100 possible employers who would have to be traced and checked.

At the top of the list was Africa Hinterland, the firm the mystery caller said supplied him with Lynne's CV. The company had been operating from a business complex at Greenwich, but when detectives went round they found the firm had gone out of business several months before Lynne had sent out her CVs.

Police also discovered that the mystery executive had called Lynne's home on four separate occasions. Twice Lynne had been at the stables and the calls had been taken by her sister Suzanne.

Nineteen-year-old Suzanne spent

Below: Police believe the killer contacted Lynne from one of these call boxes at Gatwick: he was overheard arranging the details of the meeting by a witness, who thought it was strange that someone claiming to be a high-powered businessman was using a public phone to conduct his business.

Left: Suzanne Rogers re-enacts her younger sister's last journey. Seen here outside Charing Cross Station, she was dressed as Lynne had been, and was accompanied by police officers. They were hoping that the reconstruction would jog the memories of people who had been in the vicinity two weeks before.

Above: Cab driver Thomas Reynolds recalled seeing Lynne waiting outside the station. She got into a car driven by a smallish, smartly-dressed man – a man who fitted the description of the person Lynne had been seen talking to earlier. The vehicle was a blue C-registered Vauxhall.

several hours going over the conversation she had had with the caller. There was one thing in particular that had convinced her the man really was involved with the airline business. During one phone call she could hear what sounded like the background noise of an air traffic control operations room. The caller had even broken off at one point to deal with urgent business. Suzanne had clearly heard him say: "Flight 101 – prepare to take off," before he returned to their conversation with an apology.

Business aviation connection

At Gatwick CID officers checked dozens of companies involved with business aviation charters and air traffic control. None could throw any light on who the killer might be. But appeals in the press and on TV were producing results.

A man came forward who said he had seen a girl fitting Lynne's description talking to a smartly-dressed man in a coffee bar at Charing Cross Station. The witness had actually sat at the same table as them as he waited for a train. He noticed the man chain-smoked small cigars, and he had been irritated by the way he kept fiddling with the cellophane wrappers. He was able to give good descriptions of both people.

The man was in his mid-30s to mid-40s, short – possibly only five feet four or five inches in height. His hair was brown and brushed back. He wore a smart, expensive-looking double-breasted blue suit and carried a briefcase.

Another witness – Thomas Reynolds, a taxi driver who had been waiting outside the station – came forward with details of a similar sighting. He had noticed Lynne standing on the station approach "because she looked so striking". He then saw her get into a car driven by an older man. The taxi driver told the detectives: "It looked odd. He was very short. The car almost looked too big for him." He described a C-registered blue Vauxhall – a Carlton or possibly a Cavalier.

Two boys who had been at school with Lynne had also been in the area. They too had spotted her and came forward with their account.

Detectives Auld and Bennison were certain all the sightings were of Lynne and the mystery 'airline executive'. By 12 September they were confident enough to issue an artist's impression of the man they were looking for.

Was this the killer?

In the meantime, another witness had come forward. David Sanderson, a telecommunications specialist, contacted the police with some fascinating information. In early September he had been trying to make a call from a public phone box in Crawley, near Gatwick Airport, when his attention was drawn to the conversation coming from the adjoining booth. A man was describing a job opportunity to someone over the telephone. He had asked to speak to someone called Lynne and was holding a copy of her CV. The caller was talking about a job with an executive aviation firm at Gatwick, which involved looking after businessmen on short-haul flights to Europe; France, Switzerland, Holland and Belgium were mentioned. The job carried a salary of £15,000 per annum.

Mr Sanderson told the police: "I turned to look because I could not understand why somebody with such an apparently high-powered company should be discussing a job of that nature with a prospective employee and using a public pay

Record of petty crime

Singleton was well known to local police as a petty crook, but he was better known to them as Andre Reich. He had changed his name to Scott Singleton by deed poll two years earlier. His criminal record showed a varied list of 18 convictions, mainly for small-time offences including assault, theft, burglary, car theft and possessing a small quantity of cannabis. The most serious offence was threatening a man with a loaded shotgun. But apart from a short stretch in Borstal as a teenager, he had never been sent to prison.

phone to make the call." He continued: "When I glanced to see who was speaking it was not the executive type I would have imagined. He looked unkempt and sweaty."

The date of the overheard conversation was 3 September – the day Lynne had spoken to the mystery man to arrange a meeting for the following morning. Bennison and Auld were convinced they were now getting very close to the killer. An additional piece of information from the public was about to clinch it.

A farmer from Rothersfield contacted the police to say at the time Lynne's body had been dumped he had seen a car parked on a verge in the area. Suspecting poachers might be at work, he had noted the make and registration. It was a blue C-registered Vauxhall Carlton.

The car belonged to 36-year-old Scott Singleton, who lived in a run-down council flat at Wilkinson Court in Broadfield. He was arrested on the morning of 29 September and taken to the Murder Squad HQ at Crawley police station. Like the man Lynne had been seen with, he was short and stocky. Normally clean-shaven, he was now growing a beard and moustache.

Forensic teams took samples from the carpet in his living room. They also found some unusual items in the house for a man who sprayed cars for a living: some shirts with epaulettes, similar to those worn by airline captains; a dark-coloured raincoat with four gold stripes denoting the rank of an airline captain; a pair of captain's gold wings; and a radio scanner tuned into air traffic control frequencies. It was obvious that he was interested in planes and flying.

Singleton denied knowing anything about Lynne Rogers. He said he had never met her or called her. On the day she vanished he was at the home of his estranged wife, Pat Reich, that morning. Mrs Reich confirmed the alibi.

Singleton had a false plate in his upper jaw, and police asked him if he was prepared to provide a cast of his bite impression. He refused point-blank. Superintendent Bennison and his team continued with their patient but firm interrogation. They asked Singleton when he had last been to Rothersfield. The suspect shrugged, then replied that as far as he could recall he had never been to such a place.

They also questioned him about whether he had ever pretended to work for an airline company. Singleton admitted he was interested in planes and that he had had some flying lessons and had even owned a microlight plane, but he denied ever pretending to be something to do with the business.

Identity parades

Singleton was put on two identity parades, but both the taxi driver who had seen him at Charing Cross and Mr Sanderson, the man who had overheard him in the call box, failed to pick him out.

Police discovered that Singleton used to have a car panel beating and paint spraying firm, The Casualty Car Doctor, at a business park in Greenwich. By a strange coincidence it was in the same complex as the now defunct Africa Hinterland travel company. In fact, Singleton's office and the former safari firm shared the same mail distribution system. Was that how he had obtained Lynne's details?

Suspect released

After three days of questioning, police eventually had to release Singleton. The following day he gave an interview to the *Daily Express*.

He told them: "Lynne's family have my deepest sympathy. Their hopes that the killer had been caught have been dashed.

"I have no connection with her or her family. The first time I set eyes on her was when I saw her picture in the newspaper.

"I don't blame the police, they were only doing their job, but their mistake could ruin my life. After this is over I will have to rebuild my life. It has been totally shattered."

But while Singleton was telling a reporter he was innocent, detectives were busy looking for the vital evidence they felt sure would prove his guilt.

A blue C-registered Vauxhall Carlton had been seen by a farmer near the location where Lynne's body was found. It belonged to 36-year-old Scott Singleton, a small-time crook and aviation enthusiast. He was arrested and pulled in for questioning.

There was another possibility. Singleton had a chaotic private life. He spent much of his time with his estranged wife Pat, but when he was not with her he was with his girlfriend Kim Arnold. Kim lived only 200 yards from Lynne's home in Catford. It was thought that having acquired Lynne's address Singleton may have kept watch on her house and embarked on a plot to snare the pretty teenager.

Suspect denies kidnap

But Singleton denied any involvement. Twice detectives were forced to apply for extensions to the 36-hour period that they were permitted to hold their suspect without a charge.

Fibres found on Lynne's clothes were a good match to those from the carpet at Singleton's home and some found on the seats of his car, but they were too common to be anything more than additional evidence. Bennison and Auld were 100 per cent sure they had the right man. But with his wife providing an alibi and a lack of forensic evidence, they were in no position to bring a charge. After holding Singleton for 96 hours they were forced to release him on 3 October.

Detectives then started looking into the injuries to Lynne's face. The bite mark on her chin clearly showed her attacker was a man with a missing front tooth at the front of his upper jaw. Singleton had a missing tooth in exactly the right place, but police needed a complete impression of his upper and lower jaws if they were to prove an exact match. Police set about tracking down his dental records.

At the dentist's surgery Bennison was told that Singleton had been in for treatment the previous November. He needed a new plate to replace one that had accidentally been trodden on and broken by police searching his home while investigating another matter. But the detective was disappointed to learn that old plaster impressions were not kept as there was not enough room to store them.

THE LYNNE ROGERS CASE

I'll kill y

Life! Is that all? shouts father as Lynne's murderer is jailed

man who strangled he

Evidence

Singleton's fantasy world

Scott Singleton lived in a bizarre world of make-believe. He even changed his name because he thought Scott Singleton sounded more glamorous than Andre Reich.

Detectives who worked on the case discovered Singleton was a Walter Mitty type character who thought he was irresistible to women. He told would-be girlfriends that he was anything from a retired RAF fighter pilot to an international private detective.

Police believe he had tried to snare other young women by pretending to be a company boss on the lookout for new staff. One officer who worked on the case said: "There was some evidence that Singleton had tried similar things before, but his previous victims had seen through him.

"Eventually he found Lynne, who was young and naive and was taken in by him. We do not know exactly what happened. We believe he must have held her captive for several days.

"We have to assume that he made sexual advances to her and when she resisted he killed her."

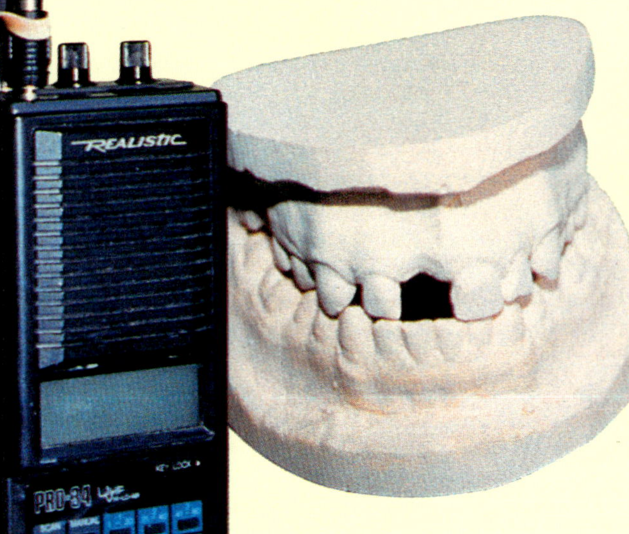

Left: The most important evidence against Singleton was the bite mark on Lynne's chin. The suspect refused to allow a cast of his teeth to be taken, but his dentist was able to provide one. Forensic odontologist Bernard Grant Sims used it to confirm Singleton's guilt.

Left: Singleton recorded air traffic control exchanges from this radio, which he played in the background as he arranged Lynne's appointment with death.

Right: Police found an airline pilot's coat in Singleton's grubby council flat. Other items, such as uniform shirts, led them to believe that he lived a fantasy life as a pilot.

DAILY EXPRESS Tuesday July 23 1992

one day

A WALTER MITTY WHO BECAME A MONSTER

Scott Singleton, born Andre Paul Reich, was sent for trial at Lewes Crown Court in July 1992. He was found guilty of murdering Lynne Rogers 10 months before, and was sentenced to life imprisonment.

The murder investigator was just on the point of leaving when the dentist's receptionist called him back. She had found the old cast of Singleton's teeth, which she had kept. She explained to Bennison that the murder suspect had been such an awkward and argumentative patient that she was sure he would complain there was something wrong with the new plate, and had therefore kept his old one.

Perfect dental match

The impressions were rushed to the murder squad HQ and carefully compared with photographs of the injuries to Lynne's chin. Bernard Sims declared them to be a perfect match. It was the vital breakthrough. On 10 October a squad of officers rearrested Singleton and charged him with murder.

Scott Singleton went on trial at Lewes Crown Court on 1 July 1992. He pleaded not guilty to murder.

Michael Seabrook QC, opening for the prosecution, told the jury: "This was a gruesome killing of a young woman who had left home to meet a man at Charing Cross full of excitement about a new job prospect.

"Five days later her body was found hidden under brambles. She had been strangled almost certainly in the process of a sexually-motivated attack which went horribly wrong."

Mr Seabrook said it was thought that Singleton had obtained a copy of Lynne's CV because his firm shared the same mail-room facility at the Greenwich business park as the travel company she had written to. Even after the safari firm had gone out of business some mail had still been arriving for them.

Two weeks into the trial a sensational new piece of evidence was presented to the court. Kim Arnold, the defendant's girlfriend, had planned to appear as a defence witness, but when she arrived in court she had a tape-recording she had found at her home. It was Singleton pretending to be an air traffic controller.

Air traffic control pretence

The recording was of transmissions between real air traffic controllers and pilots. Singleton had dubbed his own voice over the top, making him appear to be an air controller. At one point he was heard to say: "Papa 101, taxi please. Roger Papa 101, cleared to JFK."

Mrs Arnold told the court that she had remembered the tapes after hearing earlier evidence of how the caller to Lynne's home had broken off conversation with her sister to instruct "Flight 101" to "take off". Singleton, clearly flustered by the revelation, claimed that the tape had been made several years before when he was learning to fly and wanted to practise radio procedures.

Singleton's wife, Pat Reich, admitted under cross-examination that the night before Lynne went to Charing Cross she had ironed a pilot-style shirt with four-bar epaulettes for her husband. When Singleton was questioned about his coat with the airline pilot stripes, he said he had bought it when he got caught out in heavy rain. He consistently denied prosecution claims that he lived "a make-believe life of a pilot".

On 22 July the jury of six men and six women took four hours to arrive at their verdict. Scott Singleton was found guilty of murdering Lynne Rogers and was jailed for life. The fantasy world of the pretend pilot was over.

Lynne's family mourns as she is buried. Since her death Derek Rogers has campaigned to improve the rights of victims' families. He had to pay for the daily 80-mile round trip to Singleton's trial in Sussex, receiving little or no assistance. And he is still receiving reminders that Lynne's car, unused since her death, has not been taxed.

NEXT ISSUE:

Gary Gilmore – The Killer Who Wanted to Die

WHO FIRED

A bullet fired from a powerful rifle bores its supersonic trail through the atmosphere. Bullet wounds can tell medical examiners a great deal. Ideally, the forensic pathologist will be able to recover the bullet and so identify the type of weapon, as well as revealing from which direction and from what distance it was fired.

One person lies dead on the mortuary slab. Another is seriously ill in hospital. There is no question concerning the cause of their injuries: both have been shot. But where did the fatal bullets come from?

Dallas, 22 November 1963. The presidential motorcade turned out of Houston Street, through Dealey Plaza and onto Elm Street. The second car in the procession was an open-topped limousine, from which President John F. Kennedy waved to the crowds. With him sat his wife Jackie. In front of them was Texas State Governor John Connally, sitting next to his wife Nelly.

At 12 seconds past 12.30 p.m. rifle shots rang out. The President put his hands to his throat, crying: "My God, I'm hit!" Governor Connally fell forward as a bullet tore through his back. Then the President fell violently backward in a shower of blood, brain and bone.

The near-panic that followed the assassination of JFK, the

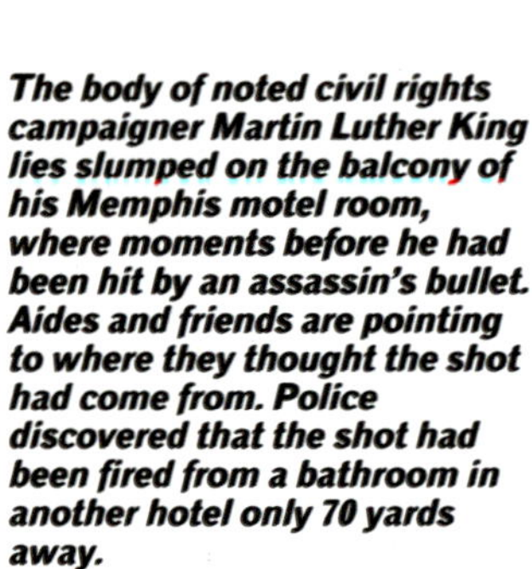

The body of noted civil rights campaigner Martin Luther King lies slumped on the balcony of his Memphis motel room, where moments before he had been hit by an assassin's bullet. Aides and friends are pointing to where they thought the shot had come from. Police discovered that the shot had been fired from a bathroom in another hotel only 70 yards away.

THE SHOT?

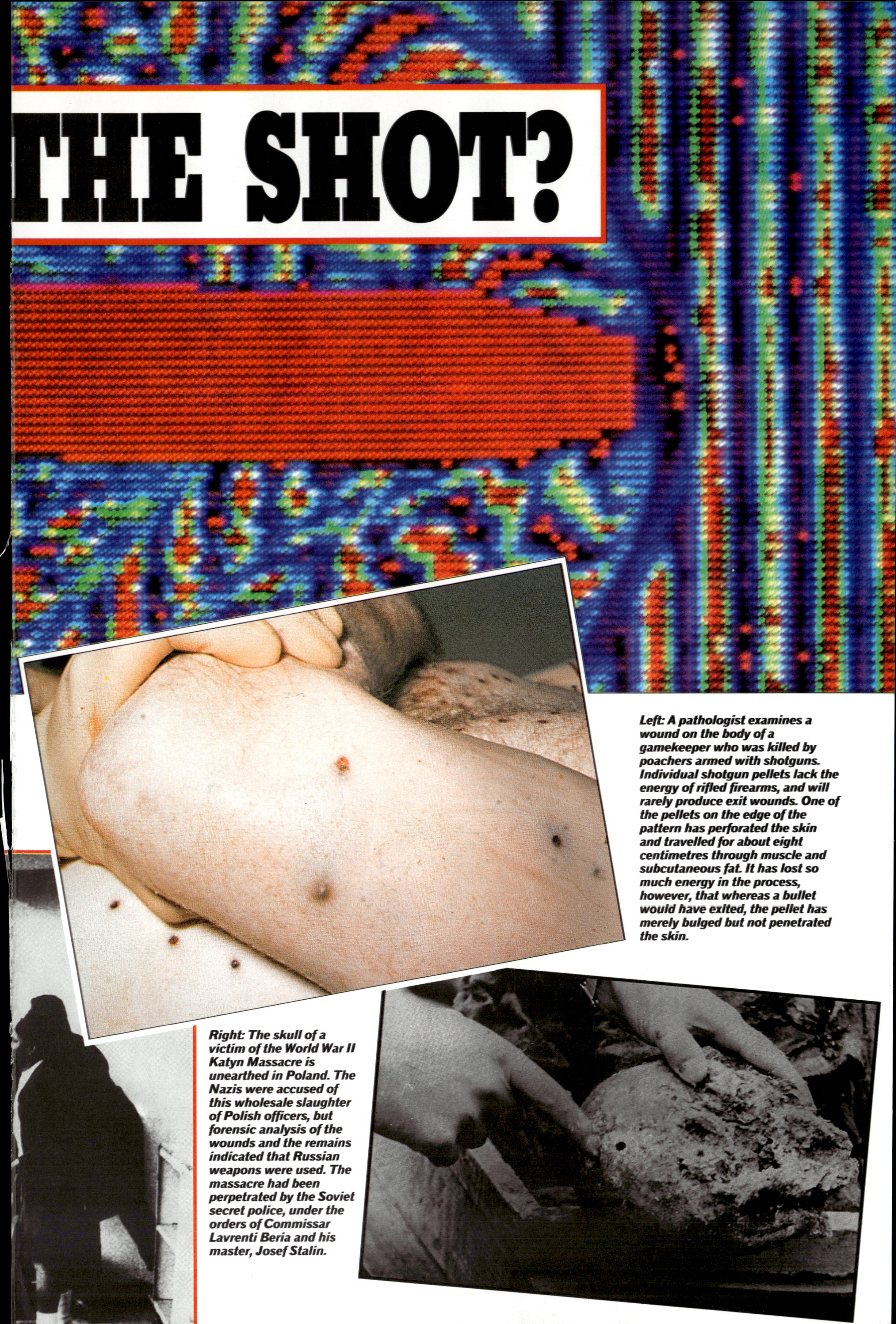

Left: A pathologist examines a wound on the body of a gamekeeper who was killed by poachers armed with shotguns. Individual shotgun pellets lack the energy of rifled firearms, and will rarely produce exit wounds. One of the pellets on the edge of the pattern has perforated the skin and travelled for about eight centimetres through muscle and subcutaneous fat. It has lost so much energy in the process, however, that whereas a bullet would have exited, the pellet has merely bulged but not penetrated the skin.

Right: The skull of a victim of the World War II Katyn Massacre is unearthed in Poland. The Nazis were accused of this wholesale slaughter of Polish officers, but forensic analysis of the wounds and the remains indicated that Russian weapons were used. The massacre had been perpetrated by the Soviet secret police, under the orders of Commissar Lavrenti Beria and his master, Josef Stalin.

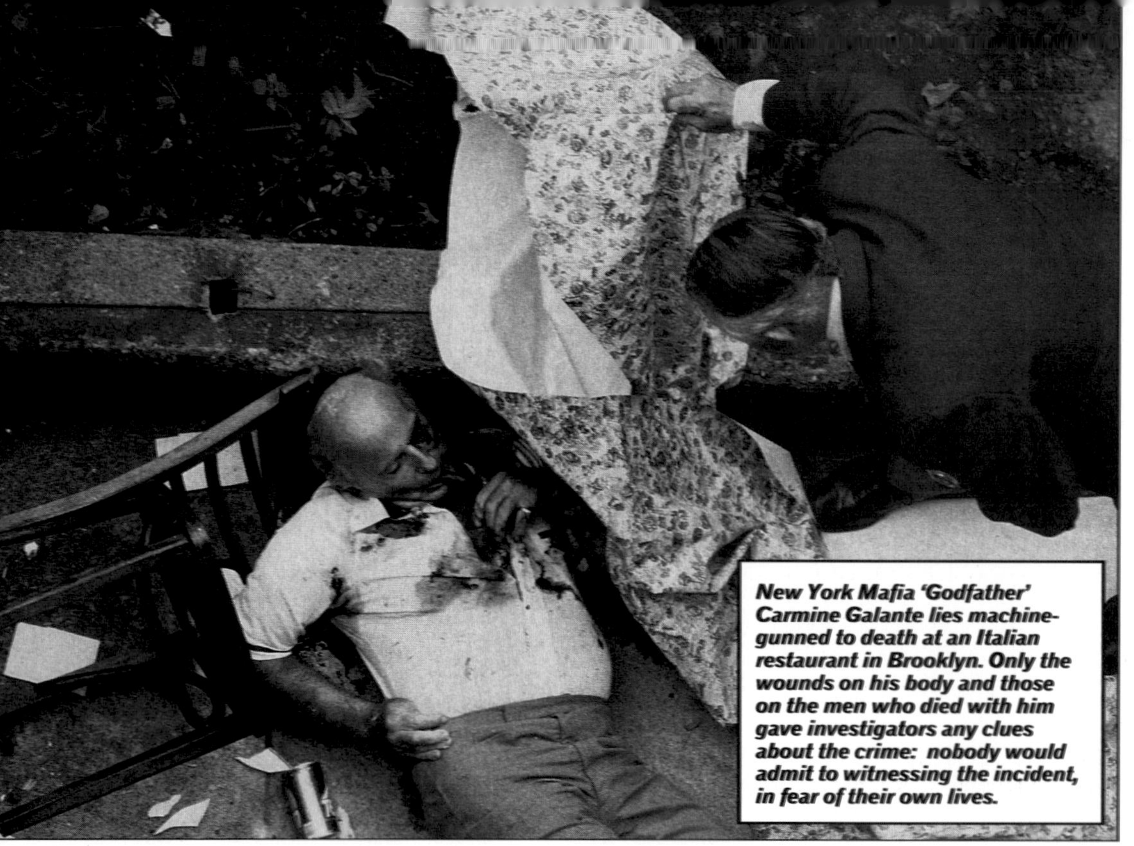

New York Mafia 'Godfather' Carmine Galante lies machine-gunned to death at an Italian restaurant in Brooklyn. Only the wounds on his body and those on the men who died with him gave investigators any clues about the crime: nobody would admit to witnessing the incident, in fear of their own lives.

Right: President John F. Kennedy is hit in quick succession by two bullets as his car passes through Dealey Plaza in Dallas. Mrs Jackie Kennedy stands up in the car, leaning over to the secret serviceman who has leaped onto the rear, and then sits down to take her dying husband in her arms.

forcible removal of his body, by the FBI, from Parkland Hospital in Dallas to Bethesda Naval Hospital in Washington, the secrecy surrounding some of the autopsy X-rays and specimens, and the disappearance of others, have all served to fuel a wealth of conspiracy theories. But much could have been learned at the time, had a pathologist experienced in gunshot wounds been involved from the start.

Pathologist's examination

A pathologist's first and foremost concern is the wound itself – not the make of weapon or cartridge that produced it. He needs to discover from what direction and distance the shot was fired; what calibre of bullet produced the wound; and where the bullet eventually ended up.

If it is known which direction the victim was facing when hit, then the entrance wound will give a clue as to the position of the gunman. And if the victim was upright, a wound that starts high and finishes low indicates a firing point above the victim.

The ease with which the range of a shot can be established varies. When a gun is fired near to a victim, the muzzle blast produces characteristic burns or powder patterning on the skin and clothing. But at longer ranges there will be no such evidence. Other factors then come into play.

The fired bullet can provide clues. A pistol round is unlikely to have been fired from more than 15 metres – American police experience shows that most pistol fights occur at less than two metres! A small 'varmint' rifle is accurate for a couple of hundred metres, while a high-powered, jacketed rifle bullet could have travelled more than a kilometre and still be lethal to its target.

But nothing is certain, and an experienced investigator will make exhaustive enquiries before coming to any conclusions.

Firearms injuries break down into two or three main areas. There is an entrance wound; a succession of tissue damage revealing the track of the bullet through the body; and, perhaps, an exit wound. The nature of each of these depends very much on the type of weapon used and the characteristics of the projectile it fires. And those characteristics can be maddeningly unpredictable.

Many things can happen to a bullet after it leaves the barrel of a gun. It may, depending upon the charge, be moving at a high velocity, or at a relatively low one. It will be spinning (at least in the case of all modern handguns and rifles), and gradually also begins to wag as it flies, converting some of its forward velocity into sideways movement. If it hits an obstruction during flight, it may be diverted; its movement may cvcn bc turned into a tumbling one.

Entrance wound

All these factors will affect the form of the entrance wound. In most shooting incidents the entrance wound is a small, clean hole with an 'abrasion collar', due to the frictional heat of the bullet where it penetrates the skin. Provided the gun was not fired at very close range – in which case the hole may be smaller than the bullet that caused it – the size of the hole provides an approximate measure of the calibre of the bullet. At long range the bullet may already be tumbling, causing a large, lacerated wound.

Bullets do not punch clean holes in flesh like they do in paper targets although, in general, the higher the velocity and power of the round the straighter its path.

Within the tissues, 'cavitation' occurs. The bullet itself will drill a relatively small hole, but the shock wave of its passage causes the tissues around its path to expand violently, forming a large cavity, which then instantly collapses in upon itself, causing serious tissue damage over a wide area.

Exit wound

The exit wound is usually larger than the entrance wound, bursting the skin outward in a star shape. If the bullet has disintegrated, partially or wholly, it may tear a big hole. However, if the skin is restricted by a belt or other tight clothing, or if the victim is up against a wall, the exit wound may be the same size as the entrance wound.

One other factor complicating the pathologist's task is that bullets do not necessarily

The shooting of a President

None of the pathologists who examined President Kennedy's body, both in Dallas and in Washington, had any experience of gunshot wounds. The Warren Commission, set up in 1964 to examine the evidence and dispel the rumours, did not interview a single forensic pathologist. It was not until 1977 that the Congress Select Committee on Assassinations assembled a panel of forensic pathologists to review the evidence, under the direction of Dr Michael Baden, New York City Medical Examiner.

In his book *Unnatural Death*, Dr Baden describes how the panel reviewed the medical and autopsy reports, photographs, X-rays and the President's clothing. One of the first questions to be resolved was the number of shots, and the direction from which they came.

Missing bullets

When examined at Bethesda Hospital, the President's body had a wound in the back, a massive head wound and what appeared to be a large entry wound in the front of the throat. X-rays showed there were no bullets inside the body, and Commander Humes, the pathologist, told the FBI that the bullet that had struck the back had gone in a few inches, and afterwards fallen out of the same hole by which it entered. This is impossible, since the cavitation effect would have prevented it. He also could not understand what had happened to the bullet in the head, and no examination of the tissues was made to determine the tracks of the two bullets.

It was not until the next day, when JFK's body had been taken away for burial, that Humes telephoned Dr Malcolm Perry in Dallas and learned that the President had undergone a tracheotomy to help him breathe. This had obscured the exit wound of the bullet that had entered the back.

High-velocity round

The bullet was a high-velocity metal-jacketed military round, and had not been distorted in its trajectory. It had, however, been diverted: it struck Connally in the back sideways on, just above the right armpit, injured his lung and fifth rib, exited below his right nipple, then entered his right wrist through the radius bone, and finally passed through part of his left thigh.

Examination of the President's clothing confirmed the type of bullet: the shirt and jacket each had a neat round hole in the back, and there were slit-like exit holes in his tie and shirt collar. Finally, when Connally allowed Dr Baden to examine his back in 1978, his wound scar was found to be two inches long – clear evidence that the bullet had been moving sideways. And the bullet that had caused the damage was found on the stretcher that Connally had been carried to hospital on; it had fallen out of the wound in his thigh.

As for the bullet that had struck the President in the head, the forensic experts made enhanced prints of the available X-rays and were able to show the track of the bullet. It had entered an inch or two below the crown, and made a massive exit wound above his right ear. The bullet had struck the windscreen pillar of the car, and was found on the floor. Dr Baden and his colleagues were convinced that there had only been two shots, and that both had come from behind.

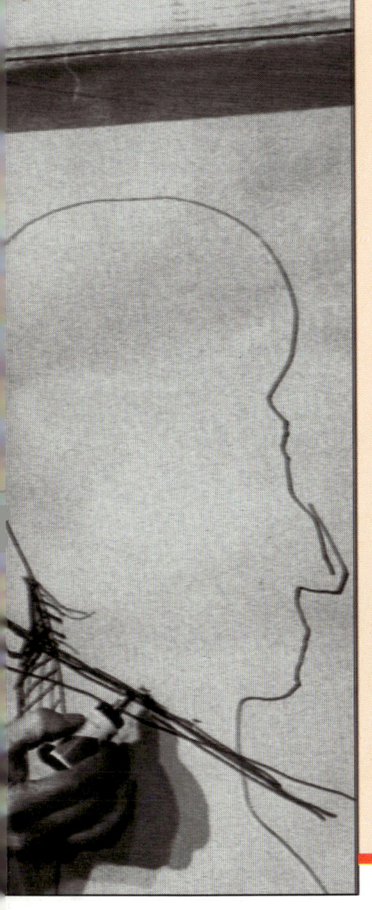

***Left:* Ten years after the killing, forensic expert John K. Lattimer demonstrated that the evidence from wounds on the President's body indicate that he had been shot by a single gunman located in the nearby book depository – which is exactly what the Warren Commission concluded had happened.**

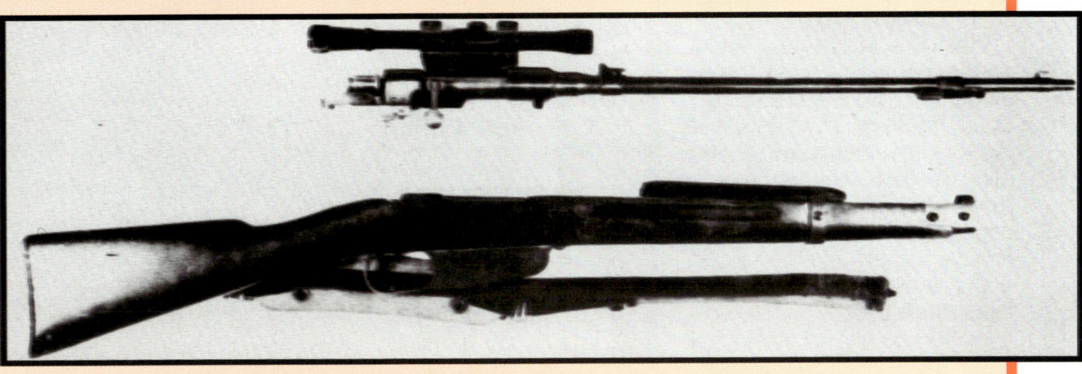

All the evidence points to Lee Harvey Oswald being guilty of shooting the President with this Mannlicher Carcano rifle. But the omission of an autopsy by a pathologist experienced in dealing with bullet wounds meant that the question would remain open for ever.

follow a straight path inside the body. Most projectiles will start to tumble after penetrating flesh. A tumbling bullet will veer away from its path, often finishing up a long way from the initial line of the shot. Even more drastic changes of direction and even disintegration of the bullet can be caused if it strikes bone. The same effect has also been observed in soft tissue, which can make a single shot look like multiple bullet wounds.

Death of a policeman

A classic example of this effect occurred in Edinburgh at around midnight on 12 July 1940. During an air-raid alert, a car containing the Assistant Chief Constable and three police officers was approaching Edinburgh police headquarters at speed when it was challenged by an RAF sergeant. The car did not stop, and as it passed by the sergeant fired his rifle through the rear window. The car stopped, the sergeant was arrested, and the ACC, who had been hit in the chin, was driven to the Royal Infirmary. He was found to have a severe facial injury and a fractured lower jawbone; three days later he died.

When the car was examined, a number of bullet marks were found. The ACC had been sitting in the left-hand front seat, and there were two holes in the licence holder and windscreen in front of him. The left-hand trafficator had also been pierced, and there was a dent made by a .303 bullet in the upper part of the windscreen frame.

Fragments of lead and nickel were found around the front seat, and on the rear seat there were portions of a .303 bullet, its tip and the cupro-nickel jacket. The evidence pointed to a number of shots having been fired, but the other police officers at the headquarters were sure they had heard only one, and no other cartridge cases could be found. In addition, the sergeant's rifle still contained four of the five bullets with which it had been loaded.

The distinguished pathologis Sir Sidney Smith examined th ACC's body. There was a shar entrance wound on the right sid of the lower jaw, and a lacerate exit wound on the left. The ex wound was three and a ha inches long, running from th chin toward the ear lobe, an had burst outward. His jaw wa smashed into fragments, but th entrance wound showed that th bullet had been intact when i struck. It had apparently jus touched the jawbone, but ha then disintegrated.

One shot, many wounds

A reconstruction of the even made it clear that only one sho

MURDER IN HAPPY VALLEY

Fatal bullet wounds do not always leave large bleeding gashes in bodies. The Earl of Errol was murdered in Kenya during World War II. He was at first thought to have died in a car accident, and it was only when the blood was cleaned from his head that a tiny bullet hole was found in front of his ear. Powder burns indicated that the shot had been fired from close range.

How a bullet kills

Although 90 per cent of all bullets are used for recreational purposes – fired at paper, wooden or steel targets, destroying water-filled bottles, smashing falling plates, puncturing tin cans, or shattering watermelons – it should always be remembered that bullets have only one purpose. And that is to kill, by punching large holes in living creatures.

In many respects bullets are simply extensions of weapons such as knives and swords. But unlike a blade, a bullet will penetrate a body at several hundred miles per hour.

Taken objectively, a bullet is almost too small to cause permanent damage. Only if it hits a vital organ, such as the heart, will it kill instantly.

But it is not the bullet alone which causes all of the damage.

Shock waves kill

Any projectile travelling at extremely high speed creates shock waves through the medium in which it travels.

In air this takes the form of turbulence. In a solid it will either bounce, bore through or shatter the material depending upon its hardness and flexibility. In a liquid the shock is transmitted equally to a wide area.

But while parts of the body, most notably the bones, will act as a solid, most of it is flesh, which is neither solid, liquid or gas.

The shock wave a bullet creates forces the flexible flesh away from

Above: A streamlined bullet passing through the air with minimum resistance will pass through a body in the same way, causing little damage. Many bullets, particularly those used in hunting, are made with soft noses. They maintain their shape in flight but 'mushroom' in flesh. Although illegal for use by the military, such bullets are often used by police for their stopping power.

Below: While the hole a bullet drills is not much bigger than the bullet itself, the energy effects cause much larger cavities to open up at least temporarily, causing immense tissue damage.

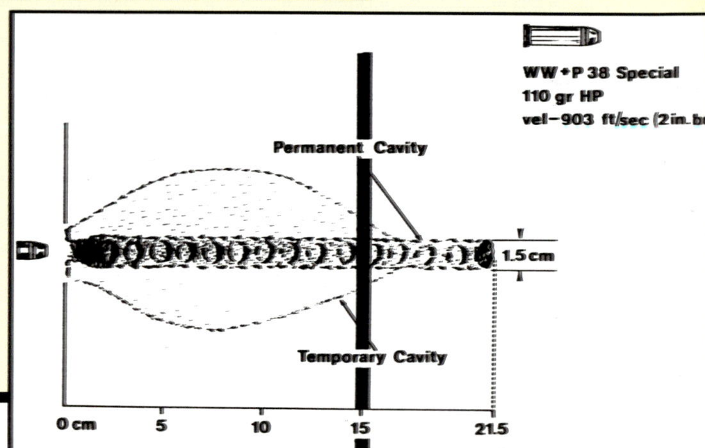

had been fired. Contact with the jaw had caused the bullet to disintegrate, and some of the fragments had produced the holes in the licence holder, the windscreen and the trafficator. The largest fragment had not continued forward in the direction of fire, but had flown upward from left to right, rebounded from the windscreen frame, and ricocheted onto the rear seat.

The sergeant was found guilty of culpable homicide but, because of the circumstances – an air-raid was expected and the country was in constant fear of invasion by German forces – he received only a six-month sentence.

Two other cases investigated by Sir Sidney Smith reveal another area in which there can be confusion about the number of bullets involved in a shooting.

In one, during World War II, a deserter was shot at from a distance of 10 to 15 yards by a service rifle, and died shortly after from haemorrhaging. There was a clean-cut entrance wound in his left thigh; the muscle was pulped by the bullet, and the damage increased as the track approached the exit, which was on the inner side of the thigh. The exit hole was about two inches across. There was a second wound, about six by three inches, in the inner side of the right thigh, and a small exit hole in the outer side. Within the right thigh, the lower end of the femur had been smashed into fragments, and minute fragments of the bullet were found in the tissues.

It might have been assumed that two shots had been fired, one from the left and one from the right. But Sir Sidney deduced that a single bullet, after penetrating the left thigh, had disintegrated in the right thigh muscle before striking the femur.

Shot by accident

In a second case a soldier was wounded in both legs and arms. It transpired that the soldier had been bending down, perhaps tying a bootlace, when a comrade's Lewis gun had accidentally gone off at a range of about one yard. A single bullet had entered the outer side of his left leg below the knee, exited on the inner side, and entered his left arm below the elbow. It had travelled through his left arm before entering his right leg, and finally passed through his right arm, emerging on the outer side. The bullet had caused little tissue damage to the first three limbs, and had only disintegrated after hitting the bone in the soldier's right arm.

Given all these factors, it is clear that it is not easy to determine with any certainty the exact direction from which a bullet was fired, nor its calibre. Analysis of any fragments will help to indicate the kind of bullet and possibly its approximate size, but the behaviour of any bullet, both during its flight and after it penetrates the target, is difficult to determine. Only very careful examination of the victim can sometimes provide the essential clue. □

its path, forming a large cavity.

The stopping power of a bullet depends upon the rate at which energy is transferred. A bullet which is slowing down quickly will equally quickly transfer all of its energy to the surrounding tissue, and the cavity it creates will be short and deep.

The cavity is only temporary, however. Flesh is resilient, so it will quickly rebound, leaving only a small permanent cavity not much larger in diameter than the bullet itself. But the effect on tissue of the violent contraction and expansion is devastating.

Torn and ruptured muscles, organs and blood vessels mean that a bullet wound has effects, often lethal, far beyond its immediate path.

A high-powered pistol bullet penetrates a block of ballistic gelatine, which has a similar consistency to flesh. It can be seen that the projectile has 'mushroomed' as it was designed to do for maximum effect, and the shock wave of its passage has produced a huge cavity, many times the diameter of the bullet itself.

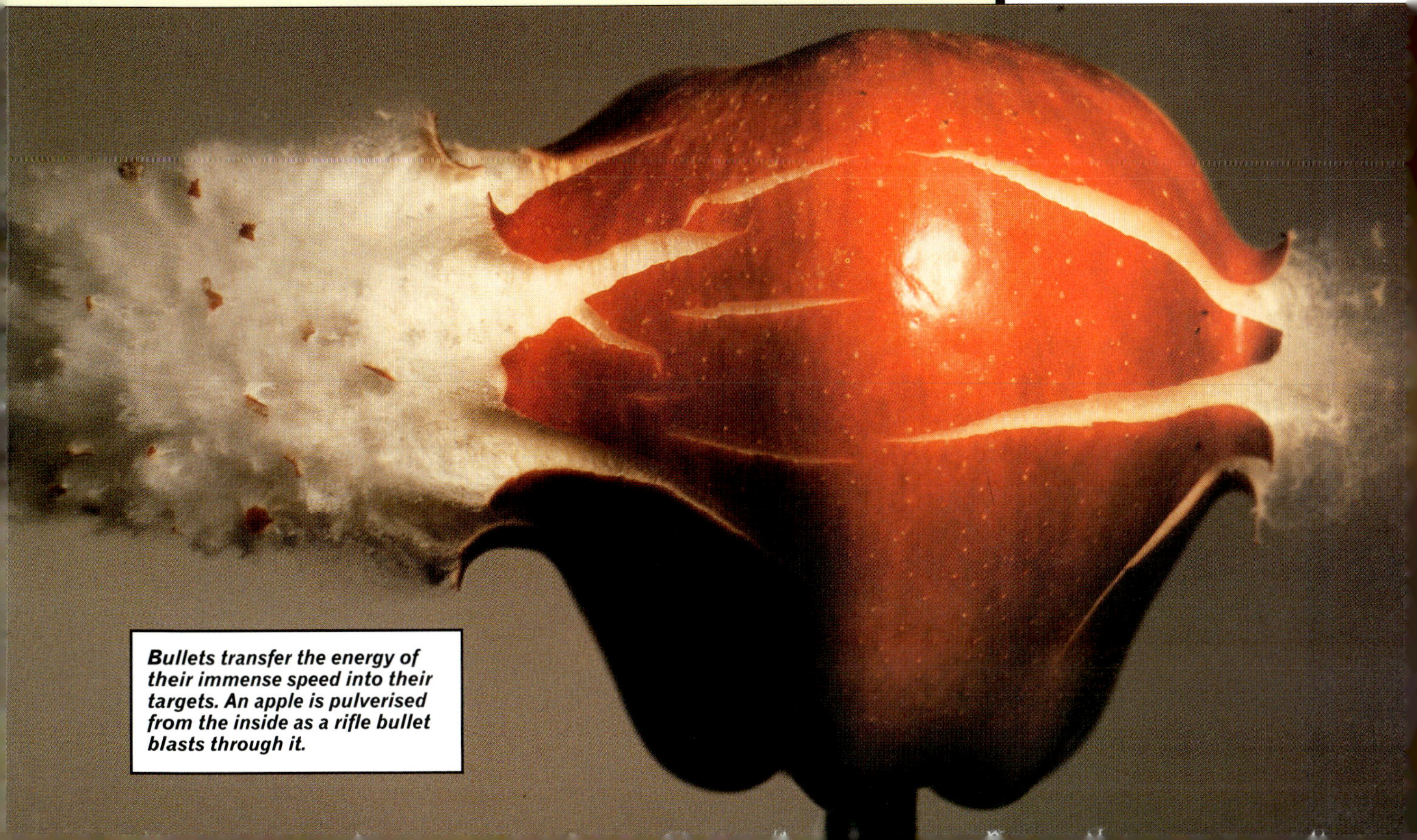

Bullets transfer the energy of their immense speed into their targets. An apple is pulverised from the inside as a rifle bullet blasts through it.

MURDER AT MADISON SQUARE GARDEN

He was the rich but violently jealous playboy husband of a beautiful young actress. One day he found himself in the same room as his wife's former lover. It was a recipe for murder.

On 25 June 1906 the Roofgarden nightspot in New York's famous Madison Square was packed with people for the opening night of the revue *Mam'zelle Champagne*.

A tall, middle-aged man with a moustache sat alone near the floor show. He was 52-year-old Stanford White. At a table nearby sat Harry Kendall Thaw, his wife Evelyn, and their guests for the evening, Mr and Mrs McCaleb.

Former showgirl Evelyn, with her alluring blue eyes, raven hair and shapely figure, drew admiring glances from everyone there that evening; and none was more admiring than Stanford White. For Evelyn had been his mistress five years earlier when, as 16-year-old dancer Evelyn Nesbit, she had been in the Broadway show *Floradora*.

Although their affair was long over – Evelyn had married Harry Thaw in Pittsburgh in April 1905 – the knowledge of it still rankled with Thaw. And that evening Evelyn, aware of the charged atmosphere, suggested that they leave. Thaw agreed. At 9.30 p.m. 21-year-old Evelyn led the way into the foyer. But by the time she reached the elevator she noticed that her husband was not with her and the McCalebs. "Where's Harry?" Evelyn asked, turning back inside.

Three shots fired

At that moment there were three gun shots. Harry Thaw had walked up to Stanford White, drawn a revolver and fired three bullets into his head and mouth. "My God," Evelyn whispered to the McCalebs, "He has shot him!"

Thaw, holding the gun up by its muzzle, walked over to Evelyn, kissed her and said: "All right, dearie. I have probably saved your life." He then gave up the gun and calmly waited for the police to arrive. "I'll stick by you, Harry," Evelyn told him as he was taken into custody.

The killing was headline news in the *New York Times*: 'THAW MURDERS STANFORD WHITE: Shoots Him On The Madison Square Garden Roof.' The paper was on safe ground to call it murder, for scores of people had witnessed the crime. In fact, most of the witnesses detested Thaw as much as they admired White. For the two men could not have been more different.

At the beginning of the 20th century society threw off the stays of Victorian morality. In the restaurants and bars of the world's great cities, people went out to enjoy themselves. And nobody enjoyed herself more than beautiful New York stage artiste Evelyn Nesbit (far left).

Above: Madison Square Garden has long been a premier entertainment centre for New Yorkers. At the turn of the century the rooftop theatre, designed by architect Stanford White, was the venue for many new reviews.

Left: On the night of 25 June 1906, Stanford White was shot dead on the roof of Madison Square Garden as he watched the opening night of Mam'zelle Champagne, a new musical review. His killer was Harry Kendall Thaw, the playboy spendthrift and husband of Evelyn Nesbit.

The playboy

Harry Kendall Thaw was born near Pittsburgh in 1871, the son of an engineer who had made millions out of steel and railways. Harry was far from being a hard worker: like his mother he was something of a social climber, a dandy given to wasting money. Yet, in spite of his unathletic character, he was prone to get into regular fights.

Thaw met 18-year-old Evelyn Nesbit in 1902. She matched his tastes perfectly: young, almost schoolgirl-like, but already experienced with men. The unmarried couple caused a scandal when Thaw took Evelyn to Europe. In spite of his mother's opposition – she thought that Evelyn was a hussy – the couple were married in 1905.

Harry Thaw was a big disappointment to his hard-working father, who in his will had slashed his son's inheritance. But Harry had always been able to manipulate his mother, and she gave him an allowance of $80,000 a year – a fortune at the time.

Thirty-five-year-old Harry Thaw was the spoilt heir to his family's multi-million-dollar fortune, a playboy whose womanising and gambling had left a trail of scandals stretching from New York to London to Paris. Stanford White, on the other hand, was America's most-respected architect, a self-made man who had designed Madison Square Garden with its theatre, restaurant, shops and prize-fight amphitheatre.

On trial for murder

Thaw's trial for murder opened at New York's Criminal Court Building on 21 January 1907, with a crowd estimated at 10,000 milling in the streets outside. A guilty verdict and the death sentence seemed inevitable. But Thaw's wealthy mother declared: "I am prepared to pay a million dollars to save his life." True to her word, the best lawyers and psychiatrists were hired to prepare his defence. Thaw's best chance of escaping the electric chair, they decided, was to plead temporary insanity.

No expense was spared in a newspaper campaign to blacken the dead man's character. White was branded a heartless scoundrel who had taken advantage of Evelyn Nesbit's innocence and seduced her. It was this that had driven Thaw to "insane" thoughts of revenge.

Harry Thaw's trial started on 23 January 1907. The prosecution was led by District Attorney William Jerome. He told the court that Thaw was a sexual sadist whose speciality was whipping brothel girls. Indeed, the madam of a Manhattan brothel, Susan Merrill, told how she could not bear the "piercing cries" that came from the private room Thaw kept in her brothel. On one occasion she had rushed into the room. "Thaw had tied the girl to the bed,

Stanford White had a small apartment set aside for his use at Madison Square Garden. Here, according to Harry Thaw, White had seduced and brutalised Evelyn when she was an innocent 16-year-old.

Below: Then, as now, there tended to be one law for the rich and another for the rest of the population. Harry Thaw, accused of murder, was theoretically a dangerous prisoner. Yet the authorities served his prison meals on china plates with silver cutlery and his own coffee service, and he slept in a double bed.

naked, and was whipping her. She was covered with welts. His eyes protruded and he looked mad."

Thaw's counsel, Delphin M. Delmas, explained away Thaw's sadistic nature by telling the court that Thaw had been born with a psychotic temperament which made him "slightly unbalanced" – not mad in the psychiatric sense, but a man who, if enough mental strain were applied, could be driven into a state in which he would not know that what he was doing was wrong. It took the form of an involuntary seizure called "dementia Americana", and was indigenous to American males who held their wives as sacred. These seizures, Delmas claimed, rendered the victim temporarily insane, and that during such a seizure Thaw had killed Stanford White.

Central to Thaw's defence was Evelyn's testimony of the manner in which her virtue had been violated by White when she was a vulnerable teenage dancer.

Evelyn explained how White had first asked her to be photographed in a "gorgeous kimono" at his Manhattan studio. The next night he had invited her to a party at his apartment; but when she arrived she found she was the only guest. She said she wanted to leave, but White insisted that she look round the rooms. In the bedroom there was a bottle of champagne and two glasses. White gave her a glass and told her to drink it.

"Drugged and ravished"

"So I drank it," Evelyn said. "Then there came a drumming in my ears. Everything began to swim around me. After that everything turned black." She told the court that when she recovered consciousness she was in bed, naked, with White, also naked, beside her – and she realised that he had taken advantage of her. White had made her swear never to tell anybody what had happened.

By this time dozens in the court room were sobbing – including Harry Thaw. Mr Delmas then asked Evelyn: "What was the effect on Mr Thaw when you told him all this?" She replied: "He broke down and sobbed and wept, crying, 'The coward, the coward!'" The 12 men of the jury looked sympathetically at Thaw; yes, they seemed to be saying, we can understand how, if you are mentally unbalanced, you lost control and shot your wife's seducer.

Thaw, it seemed, was certain to win an insanity verdict and escape the 'chair'. But District Attorney Jerome was about to elicit some damning admissions from Evelyn in his cross-examination.

Jerome asked Evelyn: "Your suggestion is that you were betrayed, after being drugged by Stanford White?"

"Yes."

"Did you not from that time on see him frequently?"

"I saw him."

The architect

Born in 1853, Stanford White's father was a respected drama critic, and his mother was from the rich Southern aristocracy. Young Stanford was privately educated, eventually becoming an architect.

After travelling extensively in Europe, White returned to New York and set up his own business in 1881. He soon became one of the most expensive and sought-after architects in the USA.

Although popular as a designer of homes for the wealthy, White was best known for his large public commissions.

White was separated from his wife, and so could happily indulge himself in one of his great passions – beautiful young women. There were rumours about his sexual habits, but they did not come to the fore until after his death.

Jealous husband

Certainly Harry Thaw believed them: he could not forget the fact that the older man had once been Evelyn Nesbit's lover. His wife had told him that White had been a brute, but evidence suggested that he had treated his young mistress well.

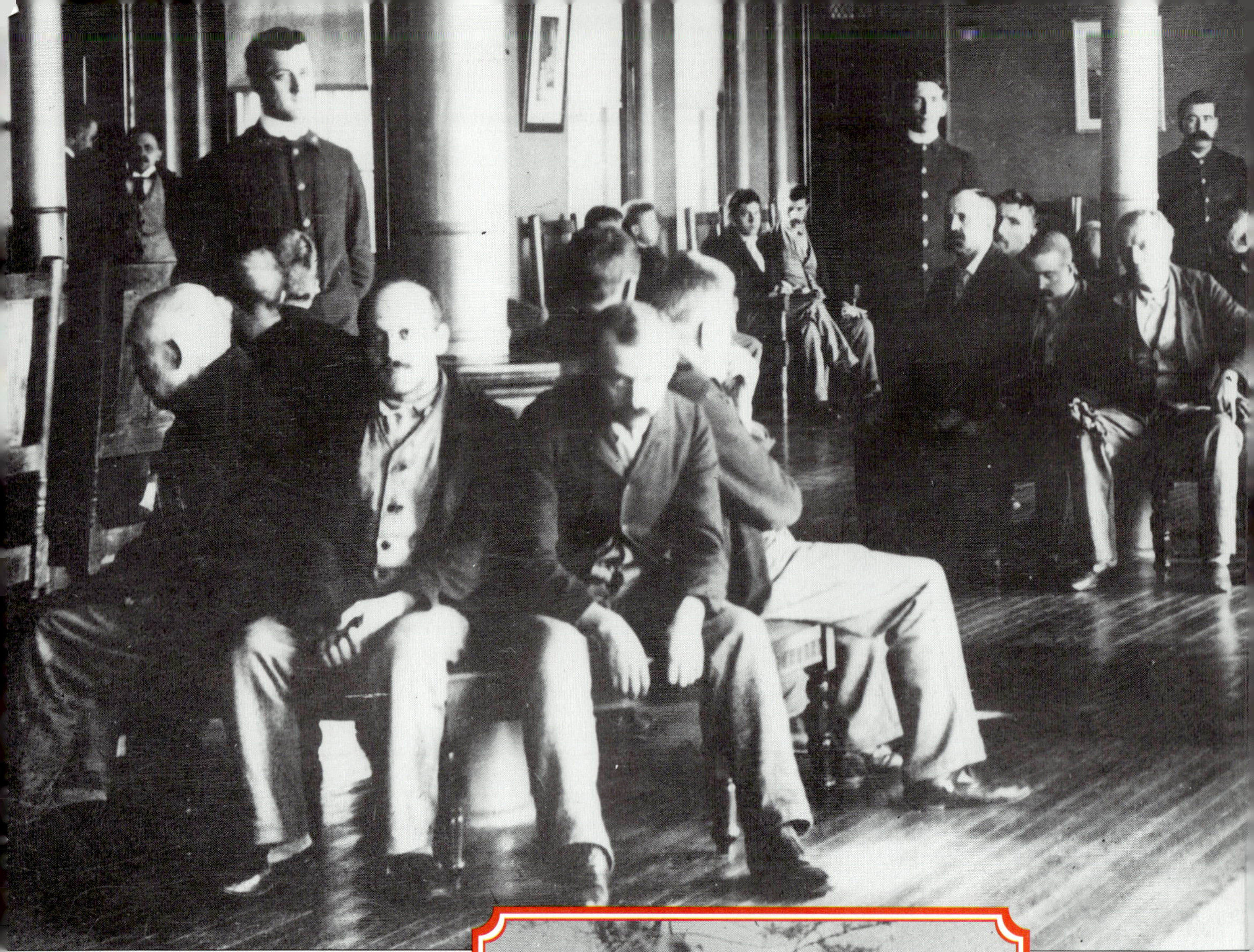

"Every week, wasn't it?"

"Yes," Evelyn replied reluctantly.

Evelyn then admitted that she had visited White at his apartment. Jerome turned the screw further: "On these visits, after the drugging episode, was there not impropriety between you and White?"

"Sometimes," sobbed Evelyn. Jerome went on to explain to the court that Evelyn had continued to have a relationship with White even after he had drugged her.

The reporters were taking down every word; Stanford White was looking less like a "brute" by the second.

Damaging letter

Then the District Attorney handed Evelyn a letter, asking her if she had written it. Her instincts were to deny that she had, for the contents were damaging to Thaw's defence, but it was her handwriting, her signature. "I think so, yes," she said.

Jerome revealed that the letter was addressed to the Mercantile Trust Company and referred to a weekly payment of $25. This sum of money was paid to Evelyn by White through the company. And she had continued to accept the money months after the drugging episode.

Evelyn, realising that this would

Above: Harry Thaw's best chance of avoiding execution was to be declared insane, in which case he would be sentenced to an asylum like the one above at Mattawan in New Jersey. The outcome hinged on one point: was he in possession of his senses when he killed Stanford White? Psychiatric evidence presented in court was sketchy, and although seven out of 12 jurors were convinced he was sane, the others would not agree. As a result, Thaw had to undergo a second trial.

Left: Harry Thaw's mother was his fiercest protector. She was at sea on her way to Europe when her son was arrested, but on hearing the news by cable she returned by the first available ship. On arriving in New York two weeks later, she declared that she was willing to spend a million dollars to save her son from execution.

Biography

The cause of the crime

Evelyn Nesbit was just 16 years old at the turn of the century. Born in Pennsylvania, she was the daughter of a lawyer who died in her childhood.

Evelyn grew into an alluring young girl, her looks attracting grown men even in her early teens. Unsuccessful as an artist's model in Philadelphia, she moved to New York in 1900, where she was an immediate success. Modelling work led to the chorus lines on Broadway, and she began to attract admirers.

Lover and protector

One of the most ardent of those admirers was 48-year-old architect Stanford White. White became her lover and protector, teaching Evelyn the ways of rich society, and even sending her to school to finish her education.

They had been lovers for a year when Evelyn, then in the chorus of the hit show *Floradora*, met rich playboy Harry Thaw, and the seeds of murder were sown.

EVELYN THAW DRAMA

Once-Famous Beauty Suffering from Poisoning

From Our Own Correspondent

New York, Tuesday: Retaining scarcely a vestige of the beauty which 20 years ago made her the toast of Broadway, Evelyn Nesbit Thaw, over whom Harry Thaw killed Stanford White, lay to-day in hospital in Chicago hovering between life and death, suffering from effects of poison.

Since a fracas in a café during New Year's Eve celebrations, in which her nose was broken, she had spent several sleepless nights, and early this morning she ran screaming into her maid's room.

When a physician arrived she was unconscious, but later in the day it was stated that she may recover.

Once a high-salaried actress, she recently descended to dancing in a cheap cabaret, but lost that employment a week ago.

Thaw, who 13 months ago was declared sane and released from an asylum, had been paying her for taking care of their 15-year-old son, Russell, who throughout to-day never left his mother's bedside.

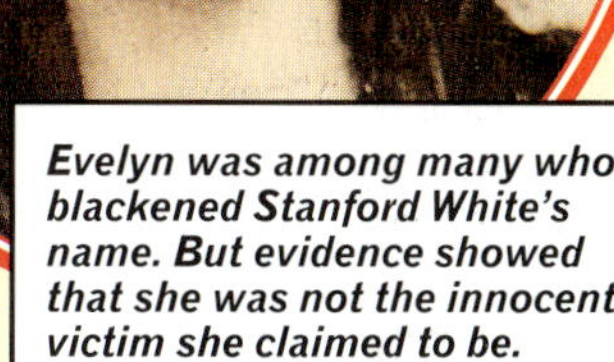

Evelyn was among many who blackened Stanford White's name. But evidence showed that she was not the innocent victim she claimed to be.

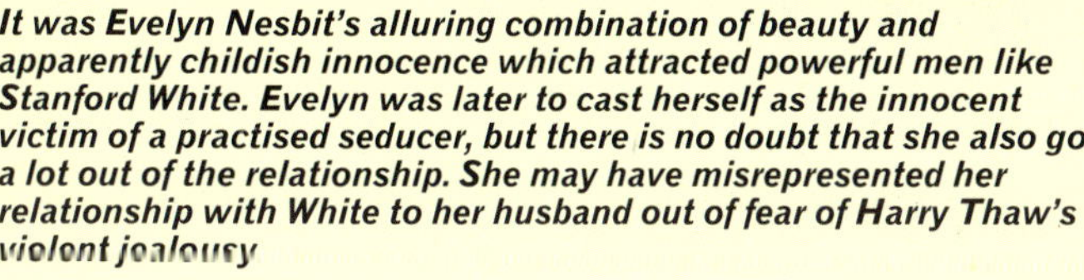

It was Evelyn Nesbit's alluring combination of beauty and apparently childish innocence which attracted powerful men like Stanford White. Evelyn was later to cast herself as the innocent victim of a practised seducer, but there is no doubt that she also got a lot out of the relationship. She may have misrepresented her relationship with White to her husband out of fear of Harry Thaw's violent jealousy

Profiting from scandal

After Evelyn divorced Harry Thaw she toured the USA as a dancer – to be denounced by women's clubs and church ministers as "capitalising her shame". But she did not invest wisely, and in the 1930s was singing for a pittance in honky-tonk bars.

Evelyn's tearful 'betrayed innocent' performance in court was exposed as just that – a performance. But she undoubtedly helped to swing two trials in Thaw's favour. As she herself would say years later: "Harry Thaw hid behind my skirts through two dirty trials."

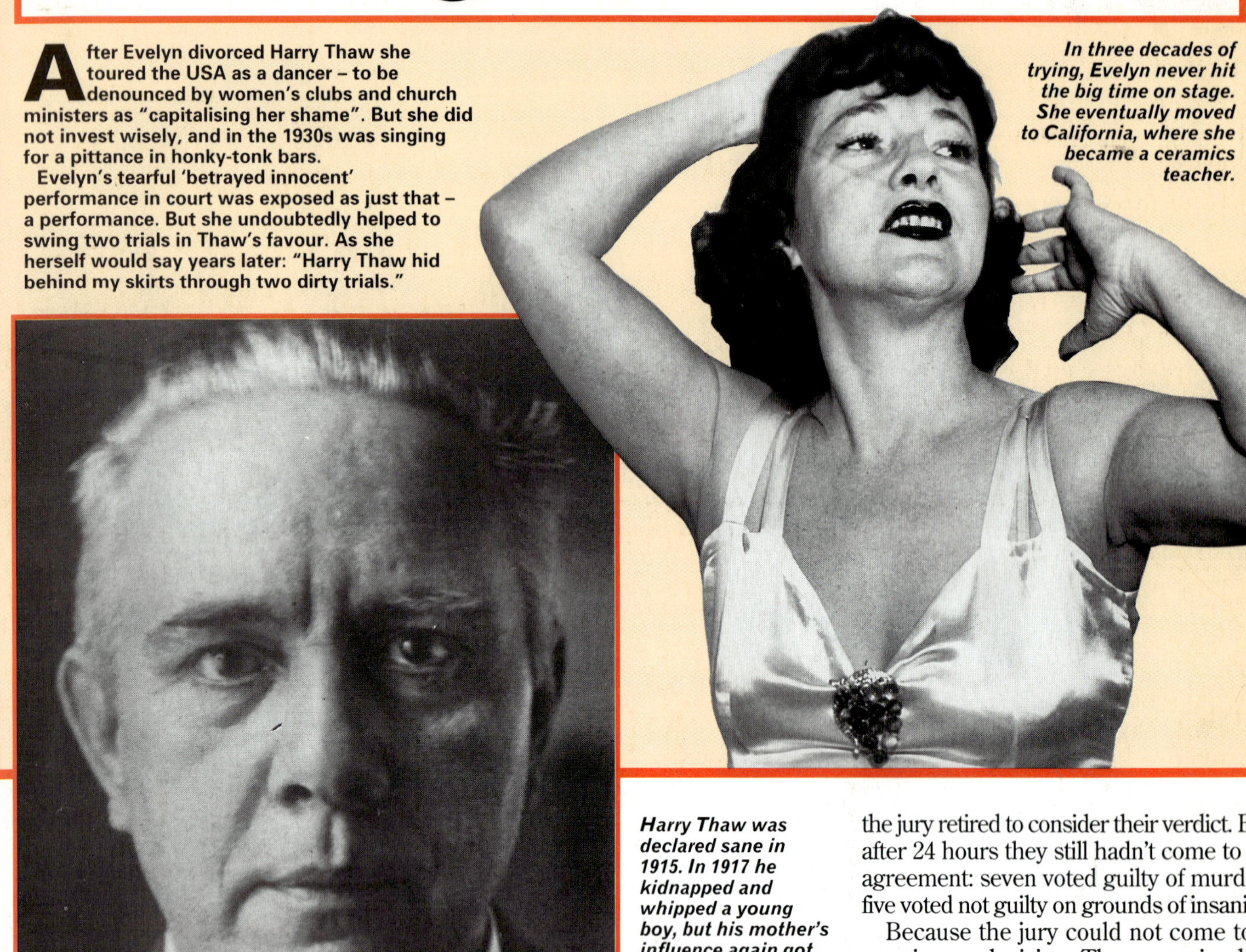

In three decades of trying, Evelyn never hit the big time on stage. She eventually moved to California, where she became a ceramics teacher.

Harry Thaw was declared sane in 1915. In 1917 he kidnapped and whipped a young boy, but his mother's influence again got him committed rather than tried. After being released in 1924, Thaw committed a number of sadistic assaults over the next 20 years.

further undermine her husband's case, said nothing. Her silence was not lost on the court. Becoming White's paid mistress did not support her story of being an innocent ingenue who had "screamed and screamed" when she found White had had sex with her while she was drugged.

Further cross-examination by the District Attorney revealed that Evelyn had also been cited as a correspondent in a divorce case before her marriage to Thaw. This was particularly damaging to Thaw's defence. He must have known Evelyn had been named as the "other woman" in the Garland divorce case (it had filled the New York papers for days), yet his defence for killing White was that just thinking about White corrupting Evelyn's innocence had robbed him of his sanity.

Jury's verdict

Evelyn had been revealed in court as anything but pure, and Thaw was revealed as a sadist. By comparison, Stanford White seemed almost a perfect gentleman.

On 11 April, after more than 10 weeks, the jury retired to consider their verdict. But after 24 hours they still hadn't come to an agreement: seven voted guilty of murder; five voted not guilty on grounds of insanity.

Because the jury could not come to a unanimous decision, Thaw remained in custody until 6 January 1908, when a second trial was held. The second jury decided that Thaw was insane at the time of the murder – and acquitted him. Thaw was sent to New York's Mattawan asylum for the criminally insane, across the river in New Jersey. He lodged an appeal in 1912, but it was dismissed. Then, in 1913, Thaw managed to escape from the asylum and sought refuge in Canada.

He was deported back to the USA in December 1914 and, sensationally, demanded a retrial. This third trial, in 1915, resulted in more banner headlines – Thaw was found sane and not guilty of murder. Thaw and Evelyn were divorced soon after. Harry Thaw continued squandering his inheritance until his death, at the age of 76, in 1947.

ISBN 1-85875-013-X

9 781858 750132

NEXT ISSUE:

Peter Manuel Eight Times a Murderer